Written by Susan Gates

Illustrated by Juanbjuan Oliver

Collins

Chapter 1

Claw was a robot. It was part of a big machine that made cakes. Claw's job was to plop cherries, very gently, onto fairy cakes. All day and night, Claw plopped cherries. That big machine never, ever stopped.

But Claw was no ordinary robot. It could see and hear. It had thoughts and feelings.

Claw thought, "I want to see the world outside. And I want to find a friend."

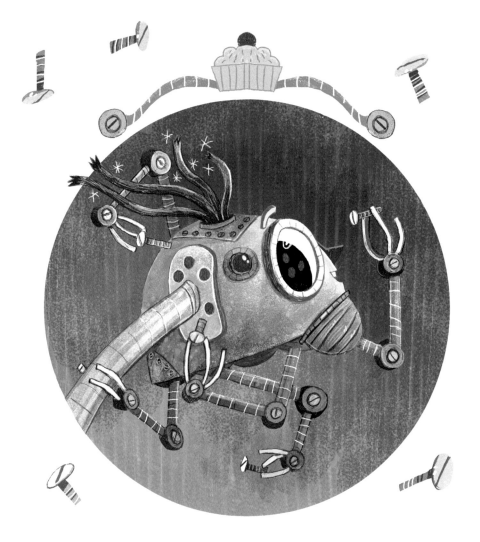

So one night, Claw decided to run away. With its long silver fingers, it undid the screws that fixed it to the machine.

"Freedom!" thought Claw as the last screw came out. Its little red eyes glowed with excitement.

Suddenly, the big machine stopped.

Sirens started screaming. Humans came running.

Scared, Claw jumped to the floor. It hid under the machine.

"The robot claw is missing!" someone shouted.

"Find it!" another human yelled. "The machine won't work without it!"

Everyone hunted for Claw. Two eyes looked under
the machine. But they didn't see Claw, hidden in the darkness.
A door opened. Claw saw the starry night outside and ran
towards it.

"There it is!" the humans shouted.
"Catch it!"

They all chased Claw. But Claw
was too fast. It whizzed through
the door and rolled like a silver
ball down the hill. It rolled
through the park gates and hid,
trembling, under a bush.

Chapter 2

Daylight came and Claw looked around the park. It saw trees and flowers and it heard birds singing.

"The world outside is beautiful," Claw thought. "I'm so glad I escaped from the machine."

A butterfly flew past. Curious, Claw trapped it in long silver fingers. Claw looked at it and then, very gently, let it go.

"Now I must find a friend," Claw decided.

Dog walkers came into the park and chatted and smiled. Everyone seemed happy. The dogs chased balls, their tails wagging. They took the balls back to their owners who tickled their tummies and gave them doggy treats.

"I'm sure to find a friend here," thought Claw.

Claw scuttled across the grass and caught a ball. It took the ball to a woman, then flipped over to be tickled.

But the woman screamed, "Help! It's a giant spider! It'll bite me!"

All the dogs started barking.

A man shouted, "Stamp on it! Squash the monster!"

Claw was a helpful, gentle robot. It didn't want to hurt anyone.

"Those humans called me a monster," it thought, bewildered. "They wanted to squash me!"

Claw scuttled off. Dogs and humans chased it. But Claw got away and hid in some long grass.

"No one here wants to be friends with a claw," it thought sadly. "I'll have to keep looking."

9

Chapter 3

There was a playground in the park. Claw saw children on swings and slides. Some were whizzing around on skateboards, shouting with delight.

"Will children be my friends?" Claw wondered.

A skateboard rolled past. Claw hopped on, scooting with its long fingers.

"Whee!" Claw thought. "This is fun!"

Claw did all kinds of amazing tricks on the skateboard. It spun on one finger. It leapt high in the air and turned four somersaults! Children crowded round, clapping and cheering.

"Cool!" they shouted.

One said, "You're a star!"

Claw's red eyes glowed with happiness.

"They like me!" thought Claw. "At last I've found some friends."

Claw started showing off to its new friends. It got really excited. It skated wildly through a football game, waving three silver fingers in the air.

Suddenly, Claw heard a strange sound. "Psssst!"

The children had stopped cheering and clapping. One of Claw's long fingers had burst their football.

"Look what you've done!" a girl shouted. "I was just going to score a goal."

"You've spoilt our game!" yelled a boy. "We don't want to play with you anymore."

Claw scuttled away. Its glowing red eyes grew dull with disappointment.

"Humans will never be friends with a claw," it decided. "I'll just have to keep looking."

Chapter 4

Claw scuttled on, keeping away from humans.

The park had a big glasshouse. Claw hid inside among the plants. It heard a girl say, "Let's go and see the spiders!"

"Spiders?" Claw remembered. That woman had called Claw a spider.

"Maybe a spider will be my friend?" it wondered.

Claw scuttled after the humans. They were staring into a glass tank.

"Look at that amazing spider!' said the girl.
"It's really big."

When the humans had gone, Claw climbed up to the tank. It saw legs slide out from behind a rock.

"It's a claw like me!" thought Claw, delighted. "It won't think I'm a monster!"

With its sharp fingers, Claw sawed a hole in
the tank lid. It squeezed inside and rushed eagerly up to
the other claw, waving its fingers in greeting. But Claw had
made a big mistake.

A furry body jumped from behind the rock.

"Aaaargh!" thought Claw. It wasn't a claw at all. And it
didn't seem friendly.

The spider leapt on Claw. It wrapped Claw up, like a parcel, in a sticky web.

Then it began dragging Claw to its den.

Claw managed to free two fingers. Using them as scissors, it snipped through the web.

Claw jumped down from the tank and scuttled away.

Chapter 5

Claw raced through the park, trying to get as far as it could from the spider. But suddenly it stopped.

Two baby swans were in danger! They were about to slip down a drain.

"I've got to help them!" thought Claw.

Claw picked the two cygnets up, very gently, cradling them in its silver fingers. It put them back on the grass where they were safe.

But the father swan didn't understand. He thought Claw was going to hurt his babies. He came rushing up and tried to peck Claw, flapping his wings and hissing.

Claw scuttled on, through the park gates and into the town.

19

Claw ran through the busy town. It dashed across a road and almost got squashed by a car. It scuttled in gutters and nearly got swept up by a road sweeper. It climbed a tree when it saw some children. Claw didn't want anything to do with children. Its glowing red eyes peered down through the branches.

"Children don't like me," it thought. "They won't be my friends."

Claw ran and ran until it reached a beach. Then there was nowhere left to run. So it dived into the sea. It swam right to the sandy sea bottom where it hid among shells and waving seaweed.

Chapter 6

Claw sat on the sandy sea bottom.

It thought, "It's scary for a claw out in the big wide world."

Claw almost wished it hadn't escaped and it was part of that big machine again, plopping cherries onto fairy cakes.

"At least I was safe there," it thought.

Then a shell started scuttling across the sand. A bunch of legs poked out.

"It's a claw like me!" thought Claw.

It saw other shells scuttling, other claws poking out. They were carrying shells on their backs like houses.

"What a great idea!" thought Claw.

It found a big shell and squeezed inside. Had it found some friends at last?

Then a pink shell
came rushing out from
the waving seaweed. It grabbed
another claw and tried to pull
it out of its shell.

"It wants that other
claw's house!" Claw thought.

The claw in the pink
shell tugged and tugged.
But the other claw held on
tightly and wouldn't budge.

"That isn't friendly at all!"
thought Claw.

Lots of claws seemed to
be snatching houses. All over
the sandy sea bottom there
were battles going on.

"I'd better get out of here!"
thought Claw. "They're going to
snatch my house in a minute!"

And, with its house
on its back, it swam up
through waves.

Chapter 7

With its house still on its back, Claw washed up on the beach. A girl and boy came along.

"Oh no," thought Claw. "Children! They'll call me a monster!" But it couldn't run away. After all its adventures, it was just too weary.

But the children didn't call Claw a monster.

The girl said, "Is it a hermit crab?" She tipped Claw out of its shell. Claw glittered on the beach.

"It's like a star," said the boy. "Or a jewel."

"Its eyes shine like rubies," said the girl.

The boy said, "I think it's a precious thing."

"It's precious," the girl agreed. "Let's take it home."

So Claw found a home with a human family.

It peeled oranges with its long fingers. It untangled phone chargers. Gently, it combed the girl's hair and the hair of her friends. It undid knots in the boy's shoelaces. It played peek-a-boo with the baby. It was helpful in so many ways.

Soon it had many friends. And no one ever, *ever* called it a monster.

The girl wanted Claw to sleep on her bed, instead of her cute fluffy toys.

One night, she said sleepily, "I love you, Claw." She switched off the light.

In the darkness, Claw's eyes glowed with happiness.

A feelings map

excited

scared

happy

sad

proud

disappointed

terrified

brave

Ideas for reading

Written by Gill Matthews
Primary Literacy Consultant

Reading objectives:
- ask questions to improve their understanding of a text
- draw inferences such as inferring characters' feelings, thoughts and motives from their actions, and justifying inferences with evidence
- predict what might happen from details stated and implied

Spoken language objectives:
- ask relevant questions to extend their understanding and knowledge
- articulate and justify answers, arguments and opinions
- participate in discussions, presentations, performances, role play, improvisations and debates

Curriculum links: Relationships education – caring friendships

Interest words: proud, disappointed, terrified, brave

Build a context for reading
- Ask children to explore the front and back covers of the book. Discuss what children think Claw might be and why its job might be boring.
- Explore their understanding of what a fantasy story is.
- Ask what they think might happen in the story. Encourage children to support their responses with reasons.

Understand and apply reading strategies
- Read pp2–5 aloud using appropriate expression. Discuss what sort of friend the children think Claw might find. Ask whether they can foresee any problems for Claw.
- Ask a volunteer to read Chapter 2 aloud with expression. Discuss how the children think Claw is feeling. Explore what they think might happen next. Repeat this process with Chapters 3 to 6.
- Read Chapter 7 aloud. Explore children's responses to how the story ends. Ask what they enjoyed about the story and what questions they have about it.